ALIEN INVASION in my BACKYARD

RUBEN BOLLING

Andrews McMeel Publishing

Kansas City • Sydney • London

PART ONE

THE PART BEFORE THE BEGINNING

A WARNING

This report is TOP SECRET, and only for the members of the EMU (Exploration–Mystery–Unbelievable) Club, for the purpose of recording its amazing adventure.

If you're reading this report and you aren't a member of the Club, you should immediately destroy the copy you are holding, preferably by explosion.

Seriously, stop reading this and either give it back to one of us, or rip it up, or put it in a paper shredder, or toss it in a campfire and use it to roast marshmallows. But whatever you do,

DO NOT TURN THE PAGE!

ANOTHER WARNING!
SERIOUSLY!

Okay. You turned the page. But I'm going to give you one more chance. And it's not because I want to keep a secret just to be cool. If the business of the Exploration–Mystery–Unbelievable Club became public, people would totally freak out.

I mean running-around-the-streets-pulling-out-their-hair freak out. There are things you are much better off not knowing. And these things are better left to the professionals. Like us. So if you are not in the Club, for your own sake, and the sake of the sanity of the world,

DO NOT,
I REPEAT,
DO NOT
TURN THE PAGE!

OFFICIAL EMU CLUB REPORT
PART TWO
THE PART WHERE WE FORM THE CLUB

You turned the page again. I can only assume you are either a member of the Club, or you are evil. And if you are evil, we will be dealing with you soon enough.

This is the Official Report of the Exploration–Mystery–Unbelievable Club, a.k.a. the EMU Club. A.k.a. stands for "also known as," and I wrote "a.k.a." so that I wouldn't have to write out "also known as," which is more time consuming.

To keep things official in this Official Report, I should start with a roll call. These are the members of the EMU Club:

Stuart Tennemeier, President. (Me.)

Eleven years old. A born leader.

Expertise: pyrotechnic explosives (well, it will be).

Career Goal: The first Major League starting shortstop to be elected president . . . of the world. And an astronaut, in my spare time. I'm a little short for my age, but I'm planning on a huge growth spurt in college.

Brian Hrznicz, C.E.O.

Eleven years old.

Brian is my best friend, so I'm allowed to say that he is one weird dude. He's super-smart, but he's nutty. Like he has to wash his hands all the time. But when things get freaky (and they do, you'll see!), Brian is always totally cool and almost never even gets scared.

Violet Tennemeier, no title.

Eight years old.

I know, having your little sister in your club is uncool, but my mom makes me include her in everything. Violet's pretty quiet most of the time, but I have to admit, every now and then she'll do something pretty amazing. And she takes almost all of the Club's pictures, which is useful. But it also means she usually isn't in the pictures. Sometimes, I'll take a turn with the camera and get a picture of her, just so this Official Report is complete.

7

Ferdinand, Sergeant at Arms.

My dog.

Okay, now that the roster of the Exploration-Mystery-Unbelievable Club has been established, I can start telling its story in this Official Report.

So, Brian and I were sitting around in my room on a Saturday last summer, bored out of our minds because Mom won't let me play video games without her permission and Brian doesn't even have video games at his house. He has gluten-free pasta at his house! We never go there to hang out.

Brian's not only my best friend, he's also my next-door neighbor. He's home-schooled, which means he's no-schooled, the lucky sea dog. He doesn't even have P.E., and whenever I'm coming home from a hard day at school, he's sitting on his porch, reading!

So suddenly, in the middle of my boredom, I got this amazing idea. I don't like to brag, but I'm pretty much known for coming up with amazing ideas.

Anyway, you know those corny chapter books where kids solve mysteries? What if we did that? We could find a mystery that's been unsolved by the entire town, and solve it by finding some clue the police overlooked, like a footprint from a boot that's only made in one remote village in Paraguay.

Brian liked the idea, so I said we'll form a club, make me the president, and we're ready to go. Brian didn't like that idea.

"You always say you're leader of all of our stuff, even though I end up doing all the work," Brian said.

I said, "First of all, that's not true. And second of all, this is totally my idea, so I've got to be president." (I'm not sure of everyone's exact words, so you'll have to take my word for it that these quotations are pretty much what people said.)

There was a lot of arguing, mostly about our Spelunking Club from last fall. Spelunking is cave exploring and is officially my favorite word. I use it all the time, even when it's got nothing to do with caves. It just sounds so spelunking cool.

Anyway, I guess Brian was still mad that I was the president of the Spelunking Club even though it was Brian's book that gave me the idea. Meanwhile, that club only lasted about as long as the argument, because we had no idea where any caves were!

This is what the first (and last) Official Report of the Spelunking Club looked like. Not too impressive.

The
World Famous
Spelunking Club

Report

by Stuart Tennemeier
and Brian Hrznicz

Part I, by Stuart Tennemeier

Stuart Tennemeir
St. Stuart
STUART

"Okay," Brian finally said. "If you're president of this mystery-solving club, then I've got to be C.E.O., which stands for chief executive officer, which is higher than president."

I said, "Fine, you're C.E.O." But what I didn't tell Brian was that my first act as president was to make C.E.O. stand for "carries everyone's orders."

So I wrote down on a piece of paper:

Mystery Club

Stuart Tennemeier,
President

Brian Hrznicz, C.E.O.

And I held up my camera to take a picture of the historic moment. For my birthday this year, I asked for a cell phone. Instead, I got a camera. That's like asking for sneakers and getting shoelaces. My parents thought this was a good compromise, and I should be grateful. That's always their strategy: They totally ignore what I want and then make me the bad guy.

I do have to admit having the camera is better than nothing.

I got another great idea: "I know! I'll take lots of pictures, and after each mystery, I'll write up a report that says what happened, and I'll include the pictures! It will be so cool!"

You can tell I'm really into Official Reports.

After looking at the paper with our titles, Brian said, "Wait, Mystery Club is a terrible name." I just was glad he was complaining about the club's name. It meant he hadn't noticed I was the first club officer listed.

"Well, that's what it is, isn't it?" I asked.

"It's more than that," Brian replied. "We'll explore anything. It's really an Exploration Club."

Okay, more arguing.

I explained it to Brian very patiently. "We don't just explore stuff for the heck of it; we explore so that we can solve mysteries!" It's like Brian thinks we're going to go off in search of the South Pole or something.

Brian would not listen to reason. He babbled, "But a Mystery Club sounds like we sit in armchairs in a drawing room and suddenly solve the puzzle by accusing one of ten suspects." At this point, I didn't even know what he was talking about.

Finally, we decided to use both names, and because Brian won the coin tosses (best of 27), his name came first: The Exploration-Mystery Club.

We left my room to go out to the backyard. We probably weren't going to find a mystery in the backyard, but we definitely weren't going to find one in my room. I grabbed my camera so that if anything came up, I'd have pictures for the Official Report. As we crossed the living room, my third-grader sister, Violet, showed up. She always seems to show up at the worst times.

"Hi, Brian. Where are you guys going?" Violet knew better than to even try to acknowledge me.

Brian said, "Outside."

Instantly, Mom called from the kitchen, "Stuart, if you're going out, please take Violet with you."

Then I made a terrible mistake. Every kid knows it's a mistake, but sometimes you just blurt things out. I said, "Mom, Brian and I are going out to talk about a club!" You never tell your parents about clubs when there's someone who might want to be included. Because they will make you include them.

"I want to be in the club," Violet said, of course.

"Let Violet be in the club," my mom called from the kitchen, of course.

"Mom, this is not a club for little kids," I yelled back. Even as I said this, I knew it would not go over well with Mom.

"Stuart!"

I shot Brian a pained look, and he shrugged his shoulders. He didn't even care about Violet being in our club.

As we opened the sliding glass door to the backyard, Violet asked, "What's the name of the club?"

"It's the Exploration-Mystery Club," I answered. "See, I wanted to call it the Mystery Club, and Brian wanted to call it the Exploration Club."

Violet said, "Oh, I want to name it, too."

Ugh. This was going very poorly. I tried to hurry Violet out into the yard, away from Mom, where I could do a better job of managing her. "Let's talk about it outside."

But this stopped Violet in her tracks. "I've got a great name. Can't I name the club, too?"

Mom walked by on her way upstairs. "Stuart, please let Violet contribute."

Great. As the three of us walked outside, my dog, Ferdinand, woke up from his nap and followed us. I explained to Violet, "Listen, we've already got two names, which is one too many."

Violet kept at it. "Unbelievable. Let's make it an Unbelievable Club." My sister had recently fallen in love with that word. Everything was unbelievable. Her friend's new coat was unbelievable. The color of her teacher's car was unbelievable. Her grilled cheese sandwich was unbelievable. It was so spelunking annoying.

"You don't call your club unbelievable," I told her. "That's bragging. You do unbelievable stuff and then let other people call your club unbelievable."

Violet wasn't buying this logic. "Mom said!" was her only reply.

Brian said, "It's okay, Violet. We'll make it the Exploration–Mystery–Unbelievable Club." He's an only child, so he's got no idea how to deal with little sisters.

PART THREE

THE PART WHERE WE FIND OUR FIRST MYSTERY

So Brian and I were in the backyard with Violet, trying to figure out how to find our first mystery. It would have been great if there were diamonds missing from the town jewelry store, but we didn't even know if we had a town jewelry store, and if we did, how would we even find out if it was missing diamonds?

And even if there was a diamond heist, we'd have to get one of our parents to drive us to the store to look for clues. And in those chapter book mysteries, there's never a mom or dad waiting in the car, honking for the detective kids to hurry up. That would just be weird.

There were definitely no murders. We live in the suburbs! Nothing ever happened around here. We realized that there was no way we'd find a real mystery.

"Maybe I should ask my mom if she knows about any unsolved mysteries. . . ." Even as I said it, I knew how lame that sounded, and I sort of stopped talking.

"The whole idea was probably stupid," said Brian.

But I wasn't going to give up. "So what if we can't find a big mystery? Maybe we should start small. Is there any mystery we can solve?"

Brian said, "You can't find your video game controller."

"That's true," I said. "I definitely had both controllers on Tuesday, but one was gone yesterday. It's not in the game basket, and it's not on my air purifier." (Yes, I have asthma, but I'm sure that in the next ten years they're going to remove that as a disqualification for becoming an astronaut. Or find a cure. Or invent computerized bionic lungs.)

Brian said, "Let's look for it. At least if we solve this mystery, we can play two-player again."

Ferdinand barked.

Violet looked bored. "This is a terrible club," she whined. "Looking around for something that's lost is not solving a mystery."

An excellent point and therefore a great opportunity to get her to quit. But I had the feeling there would be some kind of parental involvement if she did. And besides, I had just come up with a pretty good idea for how to use Violet for the club.

"Violet," I said, "how would you like to be the Exploration-Mystery-Unbelievable Club's photographer?" I knew what her answer would be; since we didn't have cell phones, my camera was the best technology either of us owned.

"Oh, okay," Violet said, snatching my camera. This worked out great! Now Brian and I had an underling to record our every move for historical purposes.

We went back inside and looked everywhere for the controller, Violet snapping picture after picture. After looking under the couch for the millionth time, I blurted out, "WHERE IS THE SPELUNKING THING?!" No one laughed. It's tough hanging out with a clueless little sister and a best friend with absolutely zero sense of humor.

"This missing controller IS a mystery," said Brian.

"That's great," I said. "But that doesn't tell us where the controller is. We looked everywhere it could possibly be."

"Well, if it's not where it could be, then it must be where it can't be," Brian replied.

We spent the rest of the morning looking in the most unlikely places: in the toilet tank; in a bird's nest; under Dad's spare toupee (that's his word for his wig—talk about TOP SECRET!).

We looked all around Mrs. Paolo's backyard until her crazy cat came out through its cat door and Ferdinand whined and ran away. "Sure, my dog has to be the one dog that's afraid of cats," I thought.

Then Brian had a scary thought: "What if your controller got into a pile of magazines and stuff and got thrown away?"

That seemed pretty likely at this point. "What a bummer. I lost my controller, and we can't solve the mystery unless we search the dump." And I was not going to search the dump. We considered defeat.

Violet spoke up. "Why don't we do a Google search?"

Brian said to Violet, "Google can't know what happened to the controller."

"Wait a minute!" I said. "What if we search what happened to other people's controllers? People misplace their controllers all the time, and if we find out how other people found THEIRS, it might help us find ours."

"Let's see if Dad's computer is working!" Violet ran into the den, very happy we were going to follow through with her idea.

Now, here's the thing about my dad. He is hopeless with computers. He thinks he's really good with them, but he is the worst. I think he isn't even allowed to bring home a laptop from work, because he keeps breaking them.

We followed Violet into the den where Dad keeps his computer and . . . it was gone! Another mystery?

I yelled upstairs, "Mom! Where's the computer?"

She called back, "Dad took it in to be fixed. It wasn't working this morning."

No mystery there.

"Figures," I said to Brian, walking back into the den where the computer was supposed to be. "I don't know how the guy does it. It was working fine last night. He's like the opposite of Steve Jobs."

Brian just stared at the desk where the computer was supposed to be, and Violet said, "Maybe we could look it up on Mom's phone."

"She told us we couldn't use her phone today because we fought over it this morning, remember?" I said.

Just then, Brian gazed up at us and said, "Look at this."

PART FOUR

THE PART WHERE WE ARGUE A LOT ABOUT A CLUE BUT IT'S NOT AS BORING AS THAT SOUNDS BECAUSE WE FIND SOMETHING OUT THAT ENDS UP BEING REALLY IMPORTANT

We walked over to the desk, where Brian was holding up a tiny red flake of something. "What is that?" I asked.

Brian squinted at it. "I don't know. It's red, flat, and irregularly shaped."

"Uh, it's basically a piece of dirt."

"Colored red? What's it doing here, on the desk in your den? This could be a clue."

"You're nuts, Brian. Why would this have anything to do with the controller?"

"It might. It's all we've got to go on. It's better than nothing."

"It IS nothing! You think you're like some kind of master detective, and you're going to figure out that this piece of lint could only come from a certain plant that only grows on a certain island off the coast of Hungary, where my video game controller is obviously being held hostage by a master supervillain?"

When I get on a roll, I can really bring it.

Brian looked at the speck. "First of all, Hungary doesn't have a coast. It's surrounded by land. But second of all, I think this thing may have come from your backyard!"

I was not impressed. "So something from my backyard is in my den. How is that going to help us find the controller?"

Violet asked, "How do you know it's from our backyard?"

"Follow me," Brian said.

Violet and I followed Brian outside. We were headed toward Ferdinand's doghouse, which is sort of run down, but Ferdinand loves to be in there. My friend Craig's dog, Fargo, has a beautiful new doghouse, but Fargo never even goes in it. I think Ferdinand spends so much time in his doghouse because he's afraid of Mrs. Paolo's cat.

Sure enough, Ferdinand was lounging around in front of his house. As we got closer, he got up and went inside. Brian held the tiny red speck up to the doghouse. "Look, it's the exact same color," he said. He pointed to another spot. "See how the paint is peeling off in flakes in certain places down here?"

I had to admit that was pretty impressive. It didn't exactly link it to a small island off of Hungary's coast (which doesn't exist), but it's pretty cool that Brian figured out where that little fleck had come from.

But still. "So what? A paint chip from our backyard ended up in our den! How is that a clue to anything?"

"I don't know." Brian kind of looked like his feelings were hurt, but he was trying not to show it. "It's just kind of odd. How would it get inside your house?"

"Maybe my dad walked by the doghouse, brushed up against it, and then went to his desk," I replied.

Brian didn't give up. "If he brushed up against the doghouse, a paint chip might end up on his pants. But how would it get up on top of the desk?"

"You're right. That IS odd," said Violet. Figures she'd only speak up to take Brian's side.

She crawled into the doghouse with Ferdinand. Good. I didn't need her out here agreeing with Brian all the time.

Brian continued, "And if it stuck to the fur of Ferdinand, same question: How did it get on top of your dad's desk?"

"Hey!" Violet shouted from inside the doghouse. "HEY! HEY! HEY!" She crawled out yelling, Ferdinand panting after her.

"What is it?" I asked.

My sister stood up and placed a tiny item in my hand, and sure enough, it was the "A" button from the game controller. A tiny gray piece of rubber plastic with an A on it. "Where did you find this?" I asked, wide-eyed.

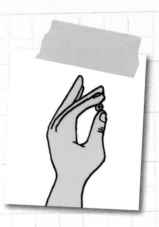

"It was way in the back of Ferdinand's doghouse," Violet replied. She smiled at me and added, "UNBELIEVABLE!"

"Ferdinand must have chewed up my game controller," I said.

"No more two-player games," said Brian.

"Ferdinand, bad dog!" I yelled. My dog barked back at me.

Mystery solved, right? For any other kids, it would have been. And if we were like any other kids, that would have been the end of the story. Case closed. And we would have lost interest in our Exploration-Mystery-Unbelievable Club.

But that's when something REALLY unbelievable happened. Brian took the tiny button from me, with a suspicious look on his face. "Wait. Is this really how the button would come off a controller if a dog chewed it up? And where's the rest of it?"

Brian crawled into Ferdinand's doghouse; we could hear him looking around. Ferdinand started barking like crazy. He'd never had so much attention inside his house.

"What?! Wow!" Brian called from inside the doghouse.

"What is it?"

"Wow!" Brian was so excited, I could see his butt wiggling.

"Brian, WHAT IS IT?"

"WOW!!"

I couldn't stand the suspense. I reached in, grabbed Brian's ankles, and dragged him out of the doghouse. He rolled over onto his back with an amazed look on his face.

"Stuart, you have got to see this." He grinned.

He just lay there, pointing at the doghouse. Ferdinand was barking and running in circles. The whole scene sort of creeped me out. "What is it?" I asked. It seemed like some kind of practical joke.

Brian just kept smiling and pointing. So I crawled in . . . slowly.

When I got to the back of the doghouse, I spotted a hole in the floor—a tunnel leading down . . . UNDERGROUND!

"WOW!"

Brian stuck his head in. "I pushed that bone-shaped chew toy into a slot in the board, and the ground just sort of slid away." Here's a drawing Brian made of the way this thing worked.

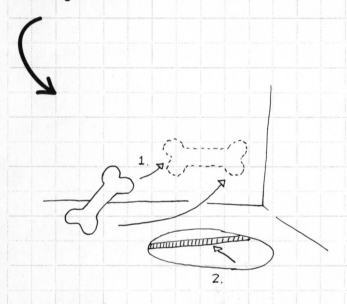

I scurried out. "What do you think it is?" I asked Brian. But Brian wasn't there.

"He went home to wash his hands," Violet told me. Of course. Because of all that crawling around in the doghouse. As stated earlier in this report, Brian has a thing about washing his hands.

I turned to Ferdinand. "What is that hole in there?" Ferdinand barked and ran around the doghouse.

As Violet crawled in to see for herself, Brian came jogging back, and said, "My mom says I have to eat lunch. And then I have my didgeridoo lesson."

I rolled my eyes. The didgeridoo is this Australian musical instrument that looks like a long, long tube, and you blow into it and it doesn't make music. Of course Brian couldn't play a normal instrument like violin or trumpet.

"Can't you skip your lesson today?" I pleaded.

"Can't," Brian responded. "I've got a video conference lesson scheduled."

I said, "Okay, whatever. After your lesson, let's go down and find out what that hole is! I think we can barely fit!"

Brian nodded. "This is an Exploration Club, after all."

"AND a Mystery Club," I was sure to add.

"But I have to go home for lunch now. Do you want to come over?"

I did NOT want to come over. But partly to be polite, and partly to show Brian why I would not want to, I asked, "What are you having?"

"Roasted vegetables and brown rice."

This was even worse than usual. I didn't even dignify this with a response. "Meet us back here after you're finished with your lunch and your lesson."

"Right," Brian said as he jogged back home.

PART FIVE

THE PART WHERE WE HAVE LUNCH (OKAY, THIS PART IS KIND OF BORING)

Violet and I went home for lunch; Ferdinand trotted in right behind us. "I'm making mac and cheese for lunch, okay?" our mom called from the kitchen.

"Yes!" we both yelled, and we ran upstairs to get supplies.

We had no idea how deep that hole would be, but we knew we'd need flashlights. I got my belt, which is supposed to be for when I wear my dress pants, but I thought it would be a cool flashlight holder.

I also have hiking boots I wear to school when it's snowy or rainy, so I put them on, and then I went out to the garage to get gardening gloves.

We ran into the kitchen and ate our mac and cheese (and baby carrots—our mom isn't THAT cool) as fast as we could.

We didn't need to run, because Brian's didgeridoo lesson took a really long time. Violet went back inside to read, and I snuck into Brian's yard and took this picture through his window (which may be illegal) because I wanted this Official Report to be complete.

I know this looks totally bizarre, and anyone would think that Brian's parents make him take these lessons, but the truth is that Brian is really into it. Note: I will NOT include in this report an audio recording of the awful sound this thing makes.

PART SIX
THE SPELUNKING PART

Finally, we all, including Ferdinand, assembled in the yard by the doghouse. Brian had brought his really goofy, huge flashlight. I set the camera on timer and got this shot of us before our mission started.

"So, what do you think is going on?" Brian asked me.

"I don't know. Is someone breaking into our house, looking around, stealing stuff, and using this hole inside the doghouse to stash it?"

"Weird," Brian said. "Why would they just steal a video game controller and nothing else? Is anything else missing?"

"No," Violet said. "I don't think so."

I looked at Ferdinand who was sort of leaning against Violet. "Our dog is such a bad watchdog, thieves are using his own doghouse as a base of operations."

Ferdinand whined.

Brian said, "I don't think it's thieves."

"Yeah, me neither," I said. "But then what's the explanation?"

"No idea. That's why we're going to EXPLORE that hole."

"In order to solve the MYSTERY," I added. I was not going to let Brian's exploration theme get the upper hand over my mystery theme.

The three of us, plus dog, had now reached the doghouse.

"I'd go first," I said, "but my flashlight is low on batteries." I knew Brian's flashlight would never be low on batteries, since checking it is on his checklist of things to do every day in case of natural disasters. Yes, Brian's the kind of kid with a checklist of things to do every day.

Meanwhile, Ferdinand was growling and barking. He was probably still mad about that bad watchdog comment. We ignored him.

"This is what we would have done in our Spelunking Club," Brian said. He led the way into the doghouse. I went next, followed by Violet. We could just fit into the hole if we slid along on our bellies. I could hear Ferdinand growling along behind Violet.

We went into the tunnel, which sloped downhill—we were headed deeper and deeper underground.

"It's really dirty in here," I heard Brian say up ahead. But I thought that even though the walls were made of dirt, they were surprisingly clean and smooth.

We kept going . . . and so did the tunnel. I never thought it would go down so deep!

The tunnel turned, and then after a while Brian shouted, "I see a light up ahead!" He sounded very relieved to be coming to the end of the tunnel crawling. (It's a good thing we never actually did anything in our Spelunking Club.)

Sure enough, as I crawled a little farther I saw the light, too, and then the tunnel emptied out into a well-lit room with a high ceiling. We all stood up . . . and couldn't believe what we saw!

PART SEVEN

THE PART WHERE WE GET CAPTURED

We were in some kind of computer room, with bright lights and weird machines all around it. The machines and computers looked homemade, like they'd been patched together from parts of other computers and electronics. I thought I recognized a part of the old treadmill Mom used to keep in the basement. The lights on the treadmill control panel were flashing and the motor was running. That old thing actually worked?

"Unbelievable," Violet whispered, and started taking pictures.

Brian walked over to a computer machine and starting turning knobs and pressing buttons. Ferdinand whimpered and trotted around.

"Brian, be careful," I warned. But suddenly, I COULDN'T MOVE MY BODY.

I was standing still as a statue, only able to move my head.

And the same thing had happened to Brian and Violet.

"I'M IMMOBILIZED!" Brian yelled.

"Yeah, and I can't move!" yelled my sister.

"That's what immobilized means, Violet!" I said.

"I knew that," she muttered. It sounded like her feelings were hurt. I was sort of sorry I had said it that way, but younger sisters can be really embarrassing.

I looked to see if Ferdinand had been immobilized too, but I couldn't see him. "Ferdinand!" I called.

If things were weird and bizarre up until then, that's when they got even more weird and bizarre.

Ferdinand walked out from behind the computer machine. He was standing upright—UPRIGHT!—on two legs, holding some kind of remote control device with his front paws.

Ferdinand pointed the remote toward Brian and then motioned toward Violet and me. Brian slid across the room until the three of us were side-by-side, like statues.

"Ferdinand, what are you DOING?!" I yelled. Ferdinand just stood—STOOD!—there, looking sad, pointing that device at us. My body felt as if it was buried in invisible concrete up to my neck.

Captured by my own dog? Ferdinand, BAD DOG!

Next, Ferdinand turned back to the computer machine and worked feverishly with his front paws, typing and pressing buttons. Wow, my dog had crazy computer skills. I had no idea.

"What do we do now?" I asked. An untrained observer might have thought I was starting to cry, but it was actually a piece of dust in my eye that I was unable to wipe away due to my immobilized state.

I looked over at Brian; he looked really upset, too. Was the enormity of our situation overwhelming him? "Brian, we'll figure something out."

"It's not that," Brian answered. "It's . . . all the . . . the crawling in dirt . . . ." He looked down at his frozen hands.

Violet called out, "Ferdinand? Brian has to wash his hands."

Ferdinand stopped his work and looked at us. Then he nodded knowingly and reached for his remote control device. He pointed it at us, pressed a button with his paw, and suddenly we could move!

Ferdinand pointed (with his paw) to a door next to the machine. Brian walked over to it, went in, then came back out and rejoined us, looking relieved.

"It's actually a very nice bathroom. One of those really powerful air hand-dryers!"

Then Ferdinand had to let me and Violet have turns. I love those air hand-dryers. They make waves on your skin like they're made of liquid!

While I was in the bathroom, Violet took this picture of Ferdinand. Weird, right?

After Ferdinand put us back under the spell of his freeze ray, or whatever that was, I asked him to take the camera out of Violet's pocket and snap a picture of us.

And this is the map of Ferdinand's secret headquarters that Brian made for this report.

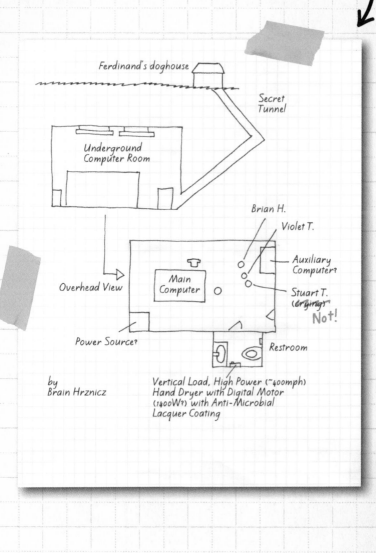

Ferdinand's doghouse

Secret Tunnel

Underground Computer Room

Brian H.

Violet T.

Auxiliary Computer?

Overhead View

Main Computer

Stuart T. (~~crying~~) Not!

Power Source?

Restroom

by Brain Hrznicz

Vertical Load, High Power (~400mph) Hand Dryer with Digital Motor (1400W?) with Anti-Microbial Lacquer Coating

Ferdinand put the camera back in Violet's pocket and went back to his computer, making doggy whines and looking more worried than ever.

Suddenly, I had a great idea. "Hey, Brian?"

"What?" Brian had to crane his neck to look at me because he couldn't move his body.

"I think the Exploration-Mystery-Unbelievable Club is too long a name."

"So?"

Violet butted in: "Do we have to talk about this now?"

I ignored her and kept talking to Brian. "So I think we should shorten the name to the EMU Club," I said.

"That's horrible," said Brian. "An emu is a dumb, flightless bird."

"That's sort of the cool thing about the name," I replied. "It's ironic." Sometimes I think Brian has no imagination or sense of humor at all. Emus are cool BECAUSE they're dumb and flightless.

Violet said, "Emus are a kind of ostrich, right? Actually, I like them."

Now Brian should have been strategizing how to get Violet to vote with him, but he can never pass up an opportunity to show how much he knows. "Emus look like ostriches, but they're actually not that closely related. Ostriches live in Africa and emus live in Australia."

"That's cool," Violet said. This was not going Brian's way. "I vote for emus!"

Brian closed his eyes like he was getting a headache. "Okay, the EMU Club can be a NICKNAME, but not the official name."

That seemed reasonable to me, but out of habit, I kept arguing. "No way, Brian! It's got to be . . ."

BAM!

There was a small explosion on the computer machine. Ferdinand ran off to the side where we couldn't see him, and came back with a fire extinguisher. He fought through the smoke and sprayed a white foam all over the spot where there were flames coming out.

Just as Ferdinand snuffed the flames out, the lights in the room started to flicker. The computer machine turned on and off, and then started shaking.

Ferdinand grabbed his remote control device, pointed it at us, and suddenly Brian, Violet, and I could move again!

"Come on, we've got to get back up the tunnel!" Brian yelled.

We had all long since dropped our flashlights, so short battery life was no longer an issue. Therefore, I felt I should be the leader into the tunnel back up to Ferdinand's doghouse. I dove into the tunnel as the lights in the room were going out. I'm not sure whether Brian or Violet was directly behind me because I was bravely leading the way out and didn't want to take time to check, but I heard another explosion, and then Ferdinand barking right behind us. My dog was abandoning ship.

PART EIGHT

THE PART WHERE WE FIND OUT WHAT'S REALLY GOING ON . . . AND IT'S REALLY BAD!

I scrambled out of the end of the tunnel and exited the doghouse; Violet and Brian quickly crawled out right behind me, followed by Ferdinand. We were all breathing hard.

We laid out flat on the grass. It was strange to be in my normal, late-afternoon backyard after everything we had just seen. Ferdinand was back on all fours like nothing had changed. Nice try.

"Ferdinand, what was all that about? Speak!"

I looked right at my dog, but he was staring over my shoulder and barking. Then I noticed that Brian and Violet were looking in the same direction, with really goofy expressions on their faces. So I turned around to see what they were all gaping at, and that's when I saw it. Violet took pictures, but she was pretty shaken up. This is the best one.

"What is THAT doing in my backyard?" I asked, but I didn't expect an answer.

Ferdinand barked. I guess he could walk and operate a computer, but he couldn't talk.

"This definitely has something to do with Ferdinand's secret computer room," I said.

"Definitely," Brian responded.

"Is that a spaceship?" asked Violet.

The thing wasn't huge like something from "Star Wars," but it was way too big to be a toy. It was more like one of those things you spin around in at an amusement park. You know those rides where you sit in a teacup or something like that, and there's a wheel in the middle, and you start off turning the wheel as much as you can because you want to spin as much as possible, but soon you're spinning too much, so you spend the rest of the ride trying to stop the wheel from turning because it's going too fast and you're starting to feel nauseous and you might puke? Anyway, that's not important. Because what happened next was really . . .

"Unbelievable," Violet whispered.

"Will you please stop saying that?" I whispered back.

"Wow," she said.

Ferdinand's barking quieted down just as a little door on the thing opened. A little ladder came out, and then, with his (her? its?) back to us, a little creature came out and climbed down the ladder. Space guy (let's go with "guy") was covered from head to toe in a helmet and red spacesuit, so we couldn't see what he looked like.

He was just about my size, but I was pretty sure he wasn't a kid. And he was carrying a little briefcase.

Space guy turned around and saw us looking at him. He hunched his shoulders and let out this weird FFFFFFFF sound! It seemed like he wasn't expecting us and was totally surprised and scared.

"What are YOU doing herrre?" he asked, in a weird, raspy voice.

I thought about responding, but I couldn't even begin to answer a question like that. I'm here because it's my backyard? Because it's my planet? Because I ran out of my dog's secret headquarters just before it exploded? Where do you start?

Brian answered: "We LIVE here! What are YOU doing here?"

The space guy unfolded legs from his briefcase, and it turned into a little desk. "We'rrre here to colonize this destroyed planet." When this guy said the letter R, he seemed to extend it for a while, like he enjoyed saying it.

Strange as it seems, it didn't even occur to me to run in and get my parents or call for help. I just stood there, trying to figure out what was going on. But I didn't get anywhere because my brain was overloaded.

Not Brian's. "Destroyed planet? Does this planet look destroyed?" he asked.

Space guy looked at Brian, considering what he had said. He reached into a pocket and took out a small device that looked like a ball with little gizmos sticking out of it. He gently raised it with both hands and let go; the space ball shot up into the air. It hovered for a few seconds, spun around really fast, then shot back down into the space guy's hands.

He looked at the space ball and then pointed up to my bedroom window, and said, "Well, that rrrroom may not be habitable."

I finally spoke up. "Uh, I've been meaning to clean up. But our planet is FINE!"

The space guy turned to Ferdinand, who kept his doggy head low, and said, "This is trrrrue. Why did you fail to send your check-in beacon?"

Ferdinand emitted a low dog whine.

Space guy seemed to understand. "Oh. Your signal device malfunctioned, and you were unable to rrrrepair it in time for your rrrregular check-in?"

Another Ferdinand whine, meaning, I guess, "Yeah."

"So, Ferdinand's job is to regularly check in to tell you that the Earth hasn't been destroyed?" Brian asked.

The space guy didn't look up; he continued working on the little briefcase desk. "You mean XL48K9? Yes, XL48K9 was placed here about 5,000 of your Earrrrth years ago, and we've been patiently waiting for his transmissions to stop. When he stops sending us the signal, we'll know Earrrrth is toast. We can do wonders with a burned-out shell of a planet."

Wow, we thought he might be an older dog when we picked Ferdinand out at the shelter, but we had no idea he was THAT old.

Brian turned to me and Violet. "Ferdinand stole your game controller so he could use the parts to fix that machine down below his doghouse."

I said, "He must have been stealing parts from my dad's computer for years. HE was the one who was on my dad's desk and dropped that paint flake!" That's why my dad was so horrible at his computer: My dog was sneaking in and stealing parts from it!

Brian said, "Ferdinand needed to fix the machine under his doghouse so that he could tell this alien that the Earth was fine! Otherwise, space guy would think Earth was destroyed and would come here to take over."

Violet whispered, "Is 'taking over' what 'colonize' means?"

I said, "Yeah, it means that this space guy wants to live on Earth instead of us." This time I said it more nicely so I wouldn't hurt Violet's feelings.

Brian continued, "When Ferdinand didn't send the signal that Earth was still okay—because he couldn't fix the machine—this guy assumed our planet had been destroyed."

I was slowly getting my courage up. Space guy was tiny and frankly not very intimidating. So I stepped up to him.

"Listen, bub. This is our planet. You're not much bigger than me, and I've taken four tae kwon do lessons. If you think you're going to take over, I'm gonna ask: You and what army?"

Space guy turned to me with mild interest. Then he spun a dial on his briefcase. As he turned it, thousands . . . no, MILLIONS of little spaceships became visible in the sky above us. The spaceships formed a thick line from my backyard up into the sky as far as I could see.

Then he turned the dial back, and all those spaceships became invisible again.

Space guy sighed. "This planet is not destrrr-royed. But since we came all this way, we may as well take overrrr. There are no weapons on this planet that could possibly stop us."

I said, "We've got tanks and atomic bombs and warplanes!"

The space guy just chuckled. "Sounds scary." Definitely sarcastic. He continued, "Now, if you'll excuse me, I'm checking whether my species can breathe this planet's airrrrr."

It seemed to me I'd seen enough science-fiction movies to know exactly how to handle this. I had to get even tougher.

I strode toward the space guy and said "Now, hold on, Obi-Wan Ka-Dopey! I ..."

It was over before I could finish saying the word "I," which is a pretty short word.

Space guy raised his space ball and pointed it at me. A green lightning ray shot out of the space ball ...

... and hit Ferdinand smack in the side! He had jumped in right between us so the ray would hit HIM instead of me!

Down went Ferdinand, wires, goop, and computer chips bursting out of a hole in his side.

My dog is a robot!

And he saved my life!

Ferdinand, GOOD ROBOT DOG!

PART NINE

THE PART WHERE WE COME UP WITH A PLAN

I don't remember who ran first, but we sure didn't discuss it. Brian, Violet, and I were in my house zipping up to my room before we knew it.

We looked out my window and saw that creepy space guy working on his briefcase-computer-desk. Ferdinand was just lying there next to him with a hole in his side and machine gunk all around him.

I couldn't believe it! Ferdinand was a robot, and now he was gone!

"Brian . . ." I turned around, and didn't see Brian.

"Bathroom," said Violet, nodding toward the door.

Brian came back into the room. He'd been in the bathroom washing his hands. "Sorry."

"Ferdinand is . . ."

Brian interrupted me. "We'll have to deal with that later. Right now we've got to figure out what to do!

"What can we do?" I asked. "If space guy figures out that he and his buddies can breathe our air, he's going to take off that spacesuit, signal his whole army down, and Earth is officially toast."

Now, someone might ask again why we didn't tell my mom, or my dad, who had just returned from trying to get his computer fixed. A space invasion seems like pretty important news. But we were sort of thinking that we could get in big trouble for causing this whole problem. Maybe if we hadn't distracted Ferdinand by poking around and then finding his secret computer room, he would have been able to signal to these aliens, and they would never have shown up.

It seemed like the best thing to do was to see if we could solve it ourselves and THEN go to our parents. Or call 911 or the Air Force.

"I wonder what the space guy looks like under that suit," Violet said angrily, snapping pictures from my window.

"Who cares if he's some disgusting blob creature, or a fungus-face? How is that going to help us?" I said. "We've got to focus!"

Brian and I joined Violet at the window. Out in the yard, a little bird landed on the fence near the space guy. He stopped what he was doing and stared at it, his body tense and totally motionless. The bird flew away, and space guy went back to work.

"Interesting." Brian said.

"What? He looked at a bird! Maybe they don't have birds on his planet." Brian and Violet were wasting their time looking at this guy when we should have been figuring out how to crush him.

Brian sat on my bed and said, "I think I've got a plan."

"Does it involve ultra-technology nano-weapons? Because these guys are SPACE ALIENS!"

"No, it doesn't." Brian had a dreamy look on his face like he was concentrating really hard.

Suddenly, he looked up at me and Violet. "We need lots of water balloons and your Super Soakers. Fast!"

I thought Brian had gone nuts. "How are balloons and water guns going to help us?"

"I don't have time to explain. If space guy can breathe our air, he's going to take off his helmet soon, and we have to be ready!"

PART TEN

THE PART WHERE WE FIND OUT WHAT THE ALIENS ARE

Violet and Brian ran out of the room to get the water fight stuff. I was going to say that this is ridiculous, but there was no one there to hear me, so I followed them out. It was my presidential decision to let Brian take the lead on this one.

Water fights were pretty much our favorite thing, so it was easy getting everything together. Violet was in charge of filling the water balloons in the bathroom sink. I ran downstairs and got my awesome Super Soakers out of the garage. These things were lethal! I mean, one pump and you could spray water clear across the yard.

Of course, there was no point in getting any water fight supplies at Brian's house. He wasn't allowed to have anything that resembled a gun in any way. His mom took a wiffle ball bat away from him when we were seven years old because he was using it as a pretend rifle in our dinosaur-hunter game!

When we were ready and loaded with all our stuff, we all went out the front door, so we could sneak around to the bushes at the side of the house and spy on the space guy.

The three of us crouched behind the bushes, watching the space guy fussing with the knobs and buttons on his briefcase. Brian and I had our Super Soakers, and Violet had a giant garbage bag full of water balloons. Violet had also brought Mom's knitting bag. "Right, like these space aliens are going to be scared of knitting needles, Violet," I thought, rolling my eyes.

I looked at my Super Soaker. It was a pretty impressive piece of machinery. "I get it!" I whispered to Brian. "They'll think these cool water guns are destructo-ray guns, and they'll give up?"

Brian watched the space guy. "No, we're going to actually shoot the water."

"Do you think he's like the witch in 'The Wizard of Oz' and a bucket of water will make him melt?!"

Brian didn't take his eyes off the space guy while he whispered, "Okay, think about it. What kind of creatures would create a robot in the form of a dog, that would be their servant, doing whatever they said?"

"Someone who doesn't like dogs. A mailman? How should I know?" I said.

We watched space guy stand up straight, bring his little space ball device up to his helmet and say, "The airrrr is fine forrrr us. Starrrrrt the invasion."

Oh, so the space ball is also a phone. I guess the lightning death ray thing is just an optional app.

"And the way he says his Rs," continued Brian, more quickly. "Almost like he's . . ."

"Purring," said Violet.

A few more spaceships became visible as they landed in my backyard!

Brian nodded and gripped his Super Soaker. "Exactly. And did you notice the way he stared at that bird?"

At that moment, space guy removed his helmet, and we saw his face! He was . . .

"A CAT?" I cried.

"Well, it's a feline creature of some kind," Brian said slowly.

"Speak English, Brian! It's a SPACE CAT!"

Brian frowned. "It's not a cat. It's an alien creature that looks and acts like a cat. Like emus and ostriches look and act alike but aren't really very related."

I gave Brian a push. "Enough! He's taken off his helmet. He knows Earth's air won't harm him. They're invading! We've got to do something now!"

The cat-alien began to unzip his spacesuit, revealing a furry, striped body. Brian said, "Wait a few seconds. Look, if we called in the Army and Navy and Air Force and Marines, they would defend Earth with bullets and bombs, and the aliens would kill them. The aliens' technology is way more sophisticated than ours."

"If you're trying to cheer me up, it's not working," I said.

"But we know something about these space aliens," Brian continued. "Think about it: When a cat isn't allowed on the couch, what do you do to train them to stay off?"

Violet said, "Melissa's mom sprays her cat with a water bottle when it goes on the kitchen table, and it jumps right down."

Now the cat-alien was almost out of its suit and another one was climbing down the ladder of the ship.

"Right," said Brian. "Cats hate water!"

Now a third cat-alien climbed out. My backyard was getting awfully crowded with these evil space kitties.

I wasn't sure this was making any sense. "But I thought these aren't really cats."

Brian nodded. "Yeah, but my theory is that if they look like cats, maybe their evolutionary path is similar, and they'll act like them."

I'd heard enough. I stood up, holding my Super Soaker.

The space cat turned and looked at me as I walked out from behind the bushes.

"THIS IS OUR PLANET, NOT YOUR SPELUNKING LITTER BOX, YOU FURRY FREAKS!"

I charged.

As I ran across the yard, a bright yellow water balloon sailed over my head toward the cat-aliens.

Oh, it was on.

PART ELEVEN

THE PART WHERE WE SAVE THE WORLD IN A TOTALLY EPIC WATER FIGHT

I don't like to brag, but I'm extremely awesome in a water fight. I mean, I'd only run about three steps in, and I'd already landed a shot right in the striped cat-alien's face.

Water splashed around him, and he let out a "ROWWWWWR!"

Brian had gotten an orange one on its side; the cat-alien arched his back, his fur stood up, and he hissed, "FFFT!"

Then Violet's balloons started landing, and these cat-aliens didn't know where to run. I was pretty impressed with Violet's arm. Direct hit on a gray one. Not bad for a third-grader.

It was actually pretty funny watching these super-genius space E.T.s absolutely freak out over some squirts of water.

While water was flying everywhere, the striped one (the original space guy who shot Ferdinand) shouted into his device: "THEY HAVE ADVANCED HYDRO-WEAPONS! REPEAT: ADVANCED HYDRO-WEAPONS!"

Yeah, that's right. We've got water guns.

Well, these cat-aliens were making a racket with their hissing and their angry meows, but we kept at them. Stripes started running in circles, shrieking into his space ball, "CANCEL MISSION!"

Space guy and his cat pals were on the run! We were going to win this thing! I thought it would be really cool to land a close-range shot on the orange guy, who was sputtering in a puddle near the bushes where Violet was. One thing I've learned in water fights is that you've got to keep shooting, to keep the enemy confused.

So I ran up to him, and said, "GET WET, WHISKERS!" And I gave a pump. Nothing. I was out of water!

Well, this gave Orange a chance to regain his senses. He looked at me, really angry, drew a breath, and pointed his space ball device at me.

I was pretty sure his device would have the lightning death ray app too.

I was dead meat.

Suddenly, a ball of purple yarn bounced by the orange cat-alien. I looked toward the bushes and saw Violet with Mom's knitting bag. I guess

Orange just couldn't resist—he bounded after the yarn ball.

Saved by my sister!

Now Brian came in for a rescue attack. A few splashes later, Orange was scampering up the ladder to his spaceship.

The gray guy got into his ship, and it almost instantly took off. I looked up, and the spaceships were now visible—and flying away!

The only one left was Stripes, who was running toward his ship to join his buddies.

I ran toward the spaceship, too, and yelled, "Brian!"

We'd had enough water fights that Brian knew what to do. He threw a fresh, fully loaded Super Soaker across the yard to me as I ran toward Stripes's spaceship.

I caught it and got to the ship just as Stripes got there.

I stood with my back to the ladder, blocking any escape, Super Soaker aimed right at Stripes. The space cat looked both petrified and furious. "We're trying to leave. What more do you WANT?" he hissed.

I narrowed my eyes. "Fix. My. Dog."

PART TWELVE

THE PART WHERE
FERDINAND COMES BACK

Stripes stared at me for a second and then looked up at all his buddies disappearing into the sky. "Oh, all rrrrright," he said impatiently.

The space cat went back to his briefcase, grabbed some strange tools (one looked like a mouse-on-a-string cat toy), and walked over to Ferdinand, still just lying there in the grass.

"No funny business," I warned him, keeping aim at his face.

Stripes shoved the parts that had fallen out of the hole in Ferdinand back in my dog and started waving the tools around Ferdinand's body.

"Is he gonna be okay? Can you fix him?" Violet asked nervously.

Stripes didn't answer, but a few seconds later, Ferdinand's eyes blinked a few times, and he jumped up and started running around, barking! It worked! Ferdinand was back!

Ferdinand saw I was busy (I was afraid to lower the Super Soaker from its aim on Stripes for even a second), so he ran to Violet and Brian and jumped all over them, licking them. Robots can slobber?

"Can I go now?" Stripes asked.

"Slowly. Keep your paws up and get back into your spaceship, you furball."

The space cat gathered his stuff and put it back in his briefcase, then carried it toward his spaceship, looking all huffy.

Wouldn't you know it, our neighbor Mrs. Paolo's cat chose that moment to wander into our yard and walk just past the spaceship. The cat saw Stripes and freaked out. Her hair stood on end, and she made that FFFFFFTT! noise. Startled, Stripes crouched to leap at Mrs. Paolo's cat. I fired, and Stripes was super-soaked!

"RRROOWWWRR!"

Stripes howled, whirred around, and ran into the spaceship, which took off without even raising its ladder.

Mrs. Paolo's cat scurried off, as the four of us stood in the wet grass looking up at Stripes's spaceship zipping away.

It was over.

Ferdinand barked and jumped into my arms, and Violet began to dance around. I said to her, "Unbelievable."

Brian stood in the middle of the backyard looking up at the sky.

"Interesting," he said quietly.

PART THIRTEEN
THE LAST PART

We heard the phone ring inside my house, and we all guessed it was Brian's mom calling for him. Brian knew he was late; suddenly, he looked more worried than he had when he thought Earth was going to become a cat-allien warzone.

"Uh-oh, I've got to go!"

Before he could run off, I said to him, "Good job, Brian. You just might get a promotion." Sometimes, as president, you've got to give your employees a pat on the back. Keeps them motivated.

But Brian didn't look motivated. "I'm C.E.O., and you're only president! If anything, I might give you a promotion! But I'm not!"

"That kind of attitude is not going to look good on your promotion report, Brian," I warned him.

Brian's face was getting red. "It's common knowledge that the C.E.O. is totally . . ." he began, but he was interrupted by my dad.

Dad was leaning out the back door. "That was your mom on the phone, Brian. She wants you home right away."

Brian began running again to his house. "Thank you, Mr. Tennemeier!"

I called out to Brian, "Go ahead home, Brian. You're dismissed." Brian stopped and turned around to argue with me again, but instead he laughed and ran home.

Wow, I got Brian to laugh.

It was an amazing feeling to go inside with Violet and Ferdinand, knowing that we had just saved the planet. Plus, tonight was taco night, which is my third favorite.

Violet and I sat down at our spots at the table just as Dad was pouring our milk. Ferdinand took his spot next to my chair. Mom sat down and said, "Did you two have fun playing in the backyard this afternoon?"

"Yeah," Violet said, and looked at me.

Dad said, "So, the computer store couldn't figure out what was wrong with my computer.

They said it must have been defective. I'm going to get a new one."

I said, "Dad, I have a feeling your luck with computers is about to change."

Dad sighed. "I hope so. It can't get any worse."

Mom said, "I thought I just heard some cats screeching out there. Did you hear that?"

"Probably just a couple of cats fighting over a mouse, Mom. No big mystery there," I said, as I sneaked a big hunk of taco down to Ferdinand, who gobbled it up.

Things were back to normal.

Except my dog is a robot.

PART FOURTEEN
THE ENDING PART AFTER THE LAST PART

So, mystery solved: My game controller was missing because cat-aliens were preparing to colonize our planet.

And that's how the EMU Club got started. Every time we find some mystery, no matter how boring, ordinary, or everyday, there's always some weird, crazy, totally freaky explanation: Why does time go slower when you're in school? What caused the grass to die in one corner of Brian's front yard? When you're going home and you have to go to the bathroom, why do you suddenly really, really have to go to the bathroom just as you get to the front door?

The answers are way more bizarre and interesting than you can imagine.

Sometimes when you're looking for a big mystery, you might not realize that there are lots of little mysteries all around you. And the closer you look at those little mysteries, the more you realize just how spelunking amazing everything around you really is.

This concludes my Official Report on our first mystery.

STUART TENNEMEIER, PRESIDENT

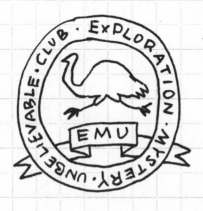

M👀RE
TO EXPLORE!
A special section with important EMU Club documents

OFFICIAL EMU CLUB DOCUMENT

PROTOCOL REPORT FOR ALIEN INVASION CONTINGENCY PLANNING GUIDANCE
By Stuart Tennemeier, President

In the case of Earth's invasion by other types of aliens, immediately send this report to the governments of the world.

	ALIEN-ANIMAL	WEAPON TO DEFEAT ITS INVASION
	Alien-Dogs	High-pitched noises
	Alien-Fish	Sun lamps, fans, possibly useworms as bait
	Alien-Slugs	Salt
	Alien-Pigeons	Statues of owls
	Alien-Bugs	Insect repellent, roach motels, fly swatter technology

	ALIEN-ANIMAL	WEAPON TO DEFEAT ITS INVASION
	Alien-Elephants	Mice
	Alien-Wolves	Elephants
	Alien-Werewolves	Silver bullets
	Alien-Frankensteins	Fire

TOP SECRET

ACCESS STRICTLY ON NEED-TO-KNOW BASIS

CLASSIFIED

FOR EMU CLUB EYES ONLY

TO: File - Personnel

FROM: Stuart Tennemeier, President, EMU Club

RE: Ferdinand

First, RE is short for "regarding," and "regarding" means "about," so this is about Ferdinand. Brian wants it noted in this report that he thinks we should not use RE since it's stupid and no one knows what it means, so you have to explain it, which takes up way more time than just saying "regarding" or even "about," but I think it's cool, and it's my report, so it's staying in. I think it's a real time-saver!

Okay, so this is a special report about what we learned about Ferdinand and what we can guess.

Ferdinand was dropped off on Earth by the aliens 5,000 years ago, which is basically prehistoric times. We looked this up on the computer, and there were still mammoths walking around on Earth then!

They gave him a machine to keep them informed on how things are going here on Earth. They were waiting for Earth civilization to get built up with skyscrapers, power plants, kitty litter factories, etc. And when it destroyed itself, they would come back and it would be easy to take over our planet and fix it back up.

So they gave Ferdinand this computer/telephone
device, and he kept sending the aliens signals
saying the Earth was not destroyed, and they
stayed away, waiting.

And wherever he went, whoever he lived with
over thousands of years, he always secretly
kept this computer thingy hidden nearby so he
could send out the signals.

Somehow, we ended up getting him at the
shelter, and he made the area under his doghouse

the secret headquarters for his machine. He's super good with computers and machines, which will be good to know in the future.

When his machine finally broke and he wasn't able to send in his signals, the aliens thought it was time to come in and take the planet. But the Earth wasn't destroyed, and that's how all the trouble started.

Ferdinand is an alien-built robot, but strangely, he's still pretty much a dog. He can't talk, so he can't tell us about being the pet of Benjamin Franklin or Christopher Columbus, or Attila the Hun, or whatever.

I did an experiment on Ferdinand and tried to look into his mouth to see if I could see any android or robot parts. But I had to abandon the experiment because of excessive DOG BREATH.

By the way, Brian and Violet and I don't know why the aliens were so sure our planet was going to be destroyed, but we are all doing a lot more recycling and we are turning off the lights when we leave a room. We're not taking any chances.

THE ADVENTURES CONTINUE!

Coming soon!
The next EMU
Club ~~mystery!~~
exploration!

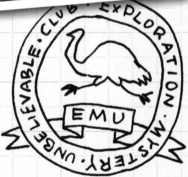

ABOUT THE AUTHOR

Ruben Bolling is the author of the award-winning weekly comic strip *Tom the Dancing Bug*, which features characters like a pre-historic ape-man, an idiot time-traveler, and a talking duck. And sometimes weird characters, like politicians.

He is the President of the Mystery Club, which was founded when he was eight years old with his friend Mike. The Club's first mystery is still an open case.

ACKNOWLEDGMENTS

I'd like to thank: Doreen Rappaport; John Glynn; Andrea Colvin; Jason Yarn; Sheila Keenan; Tim Lynch; and Adam Rex.

AND:

My parents for their love, support and encouragement; Katie, Jake and Zoe, who have filled me with joy and stories; and Andrea, my inspiration.

Andrews McMeel Publishing, LLC
an Andrews McMeel Universal company
1130 Walnut Street, Kansas City, Missouri 64106

www.andrewsmcmeel.com

15 16 17 18 19 SDB 10 9 8 7 6 5 4 3 2 1

ISBN: 978-1-4494-5709-9

Library of Congress Control Number: 2014946032

Made by:
Shenzhen Donnelley Printing Company Ltd.
Address and location of manufacturer:
No. 47, Wuhe Nan Road, Bantian Ind. Zone,
Shenzhen China, 518129
1st Printing—1/19/15